White Horses & Shooting Stars

For Sarah Harvey
—*David Greer*

To Mum again and Gianni at last
—*Chum McLeod*

White Horses & Shooting Stars

A Book of Wishes

DAVID GREER
ILLUSTRATED BY CHUM MCLEOD

Conari Press / Berkeley, CA

Text copyright © 1994 by David Greer
Illustrations copyright © 1994 by Chum McLeod
All Rights Reserved. No part of this book may be used or reproduced in any
manner whatsoever without written permission from the publisher, except in
the case of brief quotations in critical articles or reviews. For information,
contact Conari Press, 1144 65th St., Suite B, Emeryville, CA 94608.
Conari Press books are distributed by Publishers Group West.
Printed in the United States of America on recycled paper.

Cover design: Sharon Smith Design
Cover illustration: Chum McLeod
Interior production: Julian Ross and Shelley Ackerman

Library of Congress Cataloging-in-Publication Data
Greer, David, 1946—
        White horses and shooting stars: a book of wishes / by David Greer:
        with illustrations by Chum McLeod

                p. cm.
        ISBN: 0-943233-74-7 (pbk.) : 9.95
        1. Wishes—Juvenile literature. [1. Wishes.] I. McLeod, Chum,
        III. II. Title.
        GR615.G74 1994
        398'.41—dc20   94-13522
                                                          CIP
                                                           AC

1

The Lost World of Wishing

Some people always lift their feet when they drive across railroad tracks. Ask why, and they look puzzled. "I've always done that," they'll say, as if that explains everything.

Others get a restless feeling when they pass a truck loaded with hay. They have an inkling they ought to do something, but haven't the foggiest notion what it could be.

These are people who have forgotten the art of wishing. They never pass up the chance to wish on their birthday cake or the first star, but beyond that they haven't a clue what to wish on. "Oh well," they'll say, "it's just a game, isn't it? Doesn't really mean anything." But will they tell you their wish after they blow out the candles? Not a chance. It wouldn't come true if they did.

Children take wishes seriously, without even thinking about it. Then they become grownups and take themselves seriously instead.

People of all ages took wishes seriously in the days when they believed you could lose your soul if you sneezed, or the moon might disappear forever if you didn't wish on it

when it was new. Wishing was a way of making good things happen, of nudging fate in the right direction.

Anyone who wished was practicing magic. Wishers still do, when they bow three times to the new moon, or stamp their wish on a white horse, or chant a charm like "Star light, star bright."

But the most important part of magic is believing in it. Conviction is everything in wishing. If you don't believe in your own power to make your wish come true, your wish will fly away, never to be seen again. Of course, there's believing, and believing. As an Irish woman said when asked about fairies, "I don't believe in them—but they're there anyway."

Which leads to the most important point of all. If you're wishing for something possible, then it may be possible for you to do whatever you need to make it come true. The ultimate magic is not wishing, but doing.

But first you need to know what to wish on. Birthday cakes come only once a year, first stars but once a night. But, if those two are the only wishes you know, you don't know what you're missing. It's like singing in the shower and knowing the lyrics to only two songs. Whether you're warbling or wishing, variety is good.

If you're not particular, you can wish on anything you want, such as your favorite tie with the fluorescent Elvis face, or your first Caesar salad of the day (it helps to throw in a four-leaf clover). Your dinner companion may be intrigued when you close your eyes and mutter:

> *"Ketchup, ketchup on my plate,*
> *bring my wish and please don't wait,"*

but she's more likely to be smitten by your charm if you stick to traditional wishes.

The list is a long one. For centuries, the rules of wishing have passed down through the generations by word of mouth, and have been collected in volumes of folklore. These show that the rules for wishing in Kansas and Saskatchewan are very much like those in Kent and Queensland. No matter how far apart they live, people share the same ancient wishes (first stars and four-leaf clovers) and many new ones (one-eyed cars and railroad tracks). They may disagree on the details of what you need to make your wish on a white horse come true—do you have to see seven other white horses first or see a black dog afterward?—but they'll agree that a white horse is worth wishing on.

Whatever you believe, you won't have long to wait to make a wish. Ever since the world began, a first star has brought in the evening. There'll be one tonight. Wish on it.

14

2

MAKING MAGIC

Every time you make a wish, you're making magic. Bowing three times to the moon adds the strength of the perfect number. Stamping wishes on white horses uses the power

17

of saliva. Even your silence when making a wish is a magical act, allowing you to focus your concentration to bring your wish true.

The rules of wishing are easy to follow and easier to break. Temptation will tell you to share your wish with your lover. Temptation will implore you to look back at a hay truck. Well, tell temptation to take a hike. A wishing rule broken means a wish that won't come true.

The best practice for avoiding temptation is to put two Oreo cookies on a plate and spend an hour alone with them. If you can get to the point where there's still one cookie left at hour's end, you're well on your way to becoming a successful wisher.

The Spell

What better way of producing a result than commanding it to happen? "Come true, wish!" is better than nothing, but if you're truly serious, practice the three Rs. Rhythm, rhyme, and repetition add a mesmerizing power to the words you mutter.

"Star light, star bright" is the best-known wishing spell, but you can make up others on the spot. In fact, that's by far the best way, for wishing should be as spontaneous as possible.

Your images can be traditional—

Stars, sun, planets, moon
Conspire to make my wish come soon;

or more contemporary—

> *Like the bats of Jays and Yanks*
> *Make my wish a homer. Thanks.*

Trust your inspiration to guide you.

The Vow of Silence

Once you've cast the spell, you must remain absolutely silent while you close your eyes and concentrate on your wish. A good rule of thumb is to say nothing for at least five minutes after. This will give you time to eat your birthday cake or see the second star in the sky.

Above all, don't tell your wish to a soul—not to your best friend, or your priest, or your iguana. Say one word, and your wish will go up in smoke, gone with the wind, never to be seen again.

The Saliva Connection

Spitting lacks social acceptability nowadays except on baseball diamonds, where it's obligatory. Magic is as important in baseball as in wishing, and ball players well know the power of ejected saliva and tobacco juice to bring good fortune.

Saliva was thought to represent the vitality of the soul and to contain marvelous healing powers. Certainly Tacitus thought so, reporting that the Emperor Vespasian had restored sight to a blind man simply by rubbing spit in his eyes.

What aids life brings grief to the devil, and herein lies the value of saliva in the making of wishes. If you spit over your left shoulder, where the devil customarily hangs out, you will temporarily blind him. This will give you time to make a quick recovery when you've spilled the salt, and is a useful ploy whenever you're wishing to avoid bad luck, which is the devil's handiwork of choice.

Now and then, you may find yourself in a situation where spitting is out of the question. This could happen when you're in your lawyer's office, wishing his time won't cost the sky, but knowing it's more likely to if you mess up the Persian rug. When there's a pause in the conversation, stick your finger in your mouth and smack it on the palm of your other hand. Stamping your wish has the same effect as spitting, but without the mess. It's always used on white horses and is optional with other wishes.

The Perfect Number

Anyone who reads fairy tales knows that two isn't enough and four is too many. Whether it's bears, sailing ships, or wishes granted by a genie in a lamp, three is just right.

Pythagoras, who had an obsessive fondness for triangles, declared three to be the perfect number, and most civilizations have reached the same conclusion. The trinity symbolizes deity in many religions. Three represents completion: beginning, middle, and end; body, mind, and soul.

Three is also the number that gives the greatest power to any repetition of a magical act. That's why three turns up so often in wishlore as the ideal number of times to spit over your left shoulder, bow to the moon, or turn your ring toward your heart.

The Unbroken Circle

The circle is the perfect shape. Having no end, it cannot be broken. Nor can your wish if you turn yourself (or your ring or pie plate) around when making a wish.

Turning around three times, you call on the magical powers of the two most potent symbols of perfection. For your wish not to come true now would be inconceivable.

The Sinister Shoulder

The left side was the weak side for most warriors, who carried their swords in their right hands. It was also the side of God to which the damned were banished. That's why the favorite position of the devil was behind the left shoulder, where he had the best chance of wreaking havoc on the life of anyone who let down their guard.

Spitting over your left shoulder will block the devil from bringing you bad luck or standing in the way of your wish. Salt will blind him and horseshoes bean him. Give it your best shot.

26

Looking Backward

If mythology and the Bible are anything to go by, looking backward is not the way to have one's wish come true. Lot's wife looked back at the doomed cities of Sodom and Gomorrah, and turned into a pillar of salt. Orpheus looked back at Eurydice on her way out of Hades, and she tumbled back in again. The message is plain: if you glance back at a symbol of Death, you're inviting disaster.

Looking back at hay trucks, white horses or first stars after you make your wish is a temptation to be avoided at all costs. You may not turn into a condiment but you'll certainly lose your wish.

Faith

There's no room for doubt. You'll only get your way if you have the will, and you won't have the will without absolute confidence in the result. We're talking wishes, not luck.

Cats are ideal subjects on which to test the power of your faith that a wish will come true. Let's say you wish your cat (called Fats, for illustrative purposes) would come and jump on your lap. Visualize Fats approaching you and

leaping onto your knee. Turn around three times and seat yourself comfortably. So far, so good. Now fix Fats with a mesmerizing gaze while chanting a spell:

Fats, Fats, precious feline,
To my lap, cat, make a beeline.

If Fats merely looks at you like you've lost it, and goes back to licking her paw, you've omitted the one element that's fundamental to all magic rituals—you didn't believe your wish would come true. Or maybe you wished for something impossible, given the nature of cats.

Never wish for impossible things. You can't believe they'll come true, and of course they won't. Wish for money, for love, for a sunny day, but never wish for the moon—it belongs to everyone, and you can't have it. And if you wish to be the Queen of England, you better already be a princess. If you don't have a lady-in-waiting, chances are that you're something else.

3

The Wild Blue Yonder

Astronomers have a lot to answer for. The sky was a far more intriguing place when all the stars were believed to be souls that had passed to The Great Beyond. Even more mysterious

was the moon goddess with an inscrutable face and the trick of gradually disappearing with no assurance that she would ever return. People made wishes to lure her back, and wished for long lives before their souls rose up to spangle the heavens.

Even though the moons and stars have been reduced to rocks and gases in our science texts, the sky hasn't completely lost its romance. We still feel awe when a falling star streaks through the indigo, and we still make wishes on the sliver of a moon.

A wisher's heaven is the lone prairie, where you can lie in the long sweet grass, front row center to the galaxies. But if all you have is a back porch in a big city, the smallest patch of sky will do just fine. You don't need the whole sea to catch a fish or the entire sky to make a wish.

First Star

Star light, star bright
First star I've seen tonight,
I wish I may, I wish I might,
Have the wish I wish tonight.

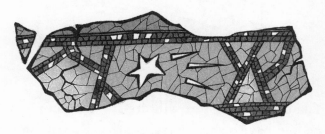

Don't hold back, shout it out. We're talking magic here, and charms only work if you say them aloud. If you're

on a crowded streetcar, so much the better—all the other passengers will follow your gaze and get their wishes, too; and you'll have done your good deed for the day.

The truth is any star will do, any time of night, but some people have a sneaky feeling that their wish won't come true unless the first star they see is also the first star to appear that night. If you're one of them, you can avoid unnecessary neck-craning by fixing your gaze on the

western sky at sunset. That's the place to find Venus, shining like a beacon long before any other star appears. As Venus was the goddess of love and sensuality, your best bet is to wish for items like romance and ripe peaches.

Venus is so reliable, it's known as the Evening Star—except on days when it's the Morning Star and appears in the east at dawn instead. On those days, Jupiter plays the role of first star, but Jupiter is a wanderer, and there's no guarantee where you'll find it. If you can't see it, just settle in, tell a ghost story or two, and wait. The stars haven't missed a single performance in the last few billion years, and they're not likely to cancel out tonight. This is, after all, the longest-running show in history.

Be tolerant of nit-pickers who tell you that Venus and Jupiter are planets, not stars. This is like saying you can't put a tomato in a salad because it's a fruit. Wishers, like world-

class chefs, achieve their best creations by not letting technicalities stand in their way.

There's only one rule you have to follow. After you've made your wish, gaze into the limpid pools of your lover's eyes or anywhere else that's handy, but under no circumstance look back at the star. If you do, you can kiss your wish good-bye.

Some people also believe that, having made your wish, you mustn't say a word till you see another star. Use this time for thinking deep thoughts, like "Where does space end?" This one thought could take you to the end of time and then some, and will certainly keep you going till Orion or the Big Dipper comes into view.

Shooting Stars

Shooting stars move so fast, you'll miss them if you blink. To learn how not to blink, spend some time with a frog. Frogs spend all night looking at the sky, hardly ever blinking. Some frogs have been known to turn into princes, which is probably more than you can say for yourself. So,

who can tell what the rewards might be of squatting in a pond with your eyelids always open?

Wishing on stars originated with the belief that every time a person dies, a new star appears in the sky, and every shooting star is on its way to earth to give life to a new-born child.

Once you see a shooting star, you have to frame it with your hands before it disappears. You may wonder how it's possible to see a shooting star, whip your hands across the sky, and frame the star—all in the space of about half a second. Rigorous training is the answer. Practice on a light bulb. After several days, you'll be ready to try this skill on moving objects, like the heads of pedestrians passing by your window.

Alternatively, you might conclude (probably correctly) that this rule was devised by the Spanish Inquisition in consultation with a team of astronomers. In which case, you might just decide to wish on any shooting star you happen to see, keeping your hands free for important tasks such as excavation of popcorn boxes.

New Moons

What's silvery and round, with a face on one side? Moons and silver dollars. Ancient alchemists said that if you turned a piece of silver in your pocket while looking at the new moon, the money would grow as the moon grew. But

then taxes and credit cards were invented, alchemists retrained as stockbrokers, and silver seemed to shrink no matter what people did to it. All in all, wishes are more reliable. They're also tax-free.

The moon is a blessing for near-sighted people who get tired of squinting at stars. The problem with the moon is that there's only one of it, unless you're on a different planet.

To our ancestors, the moon was a comforting companion when its face was full and bright, but also a fickle

42

one with an unsettling habit of fading away to nothing at regular intervals, casting the earth into an eerie blackness welcomed only by cats. After a couple of nights on the lam, the moon would return, sliver by excruciatingly slow sliver. People wished fervently for the moon to be full again, and used an assortment of magical charms in an effort to speed up the process. Eventually they gave up on the moon and found other sources of light, but the habit of wishing remains.

Don't waste your effort on the old moon, which looks like the letter C. Only the new moon will do, with a curve like a D, as in Diana, the Roman moon goddess who hunted the clouds. Now for the magic. To give your wish the power it needs, bow or curtsy three times in the direction of the moon, or throw it three kisses. Remember, three's a very magical number.

43

Full Moons

There are two important exceptions to the rule that you can only wish on the new moon. The first full moon of summer is always good for a wish, as is any blue moon. One you'll see once a year, the other not so often—maybe once in a blue moon.

Blue moons are as rare as two full moons in a month. In fact, some people call the second full moon in a month a blue moon, and wish on it with abandon.

Then there are the purists. No abandon for them, thank you very much. They wait for the appearance of a true blue moon, without the quotation marks, and they have to wait till the cows come home plus a few extra years.

Moons that really look blue are caused by smoke or ash

filling the upper atmosphere after a giant forest fire or volcanic eruption. Wish big when you see one—you won't get another chance in a very long time. If you're seeing blue moons more often than that, it's because you're wearing sunglasses at night. You've chosen to make all your wishes come true by trying to be cool. Good luck, and may the wind be always at your backside.

4

THE GREAT OUTDOORS

Whether you live in the city or the woods, whether your home is a cottage or a condo, there are always wishes near your doorstep. Every vacant lot has a four-leaf clover. If you

47

don't have the patience to find it, head for an unmown lawn where the dandelion puffs are thick as stars, or find an uncut meadow with a horse as white as the moon. And if that doesn't do the trick, wish on the first of anything you see that marks the turning of the seasons—first robin, first strawberry, first pumpkin, first snowflake.

White Horses

White horse, white horse
Lucky, lucky me.
White horse, white horse
Bring my wish to me.

No cheating here. Unicorns don't count. It has to be a

horse, and it has to be white, or at least piebald. Piebald horses aren't bald, they're white and one other color.

Once you're certain it's a white or piebald horse, make your wish and stamp it. Do this by wetting your thumb in your mouth, smacking it on the palm of your other hand, and then hitting the palm with your fist. Stamping a wish is like stamping a letter—it sends it to the right place.

Some people will tell you that your wish won't come true until a) you have stamped wishes on a hundred white horses, or b) you see a black dog, or c) you see a red-haired woman. In any group of wishers, you'll find nit-pickers who'll try and argue your ear off about proper technique. Treat them with the utmost respect, and don't pay any attention to what they say.

However, if a white horse takes you aside and tells you something, listen up. White horses have always been treated with special respect. In ancient mythology, white horses were the chosen steeds of the gods. White horses have also been the pick of more sinister characters, like a Horseman of the Apocalypse, who went by the name of Death. With riders like these, white horses developed a reputation. Wishing on them was like knocking on wood—it kept you safe from whatever invisible rider the horse might carry.

Be careful not to look at a white horse the wrong way when you're making a wish. This isn't because the horse might take offense—horses can get surly for any of a hundred reasons, but being stared at isn't one of them. The problem is your wish will never come true if you look at the horse's tail. The safest approach is to look every white horse in the mouth and pack a bunch of sugar cubes.

Now comes the hard part. Having made your wish, you must turn away and not look back, or your wish will turn to dust. If you're looking at the horse from the window of a speeding car, this won't be a problem—just fix your gaze on the dashboard till you pass a bend in the road. If you're nose to nose with the horse, your only option is a U-turn and a long walk, preferably without apples sticking out of your back pocket.

If you see a white horse with a red-haired woman on its back, wish like crazy. This sight is almost guaranteed to make your wish come true. Red-haired women are about seven times as lucky as a horseshoe, unless they don't like you, in which case they're about seven times as unlucky as a black cat crossing your path.

White Mustangs

White horses steer clear of cities as a rule. They prefer alfalfa fields, far from the madding crowd. Fortunately, there's an urban alternative—the white Mustang. (You're also in luck if you spot a white or piebald Pinto.)

Wish to your heart's content, being careful not to glance at the taillights. If there's a red-haired driver inside and one headlight is out, you've hit the equivalent of triple cherries on the one-armed bandit. Wish for the jackpot.

Horseshoes

    To make a wish on a horseshoe, you need to throw it. This wasn't a problem when horseshoes were a dime a dozen along roadsides, in the days when horses did more than decorate fields and run for the roses. Life for wishers has become far more complicated since the invention of automobiles. Nowadays, the most likely place to find a

horseshoe is on the hoof of a horse. Unless you know this horse intimately, you would be wise not to borrow its shoe.

Wishes on horseshoes have a lot going for them, however, and it'll be worth your while to keep looking. In the days when blacksmiths first learned to make magic with fire and sparks and the occasional curse, anyone who discovered a piece of iron was bound to have good fortune. And when the blacksmith bent the white-hot iron into a shape like the new moon, which symbolized fertility and growth, the resulting horseshoe carried huge magical powers.

If all your searches for horseshoes prove futile, find a house that's being torn down and put dibs on the horseshoe nailed for luck over the doorway. To make your wish, take the shoe in your right hand and throw it backward over your left shoulder. That's where the devil was believed to

lurk, waiting to do mischief to you. If your aim is good, you'll hit the devil and not the owner of the house.

Now go look at the horseshoe. If it landed with its prongs facing up, your wish will come true. If not, clear out fast. Not only is your wish a goner, but the devil is about to wake up with a headache and a bad attitude.

Rainbows

When you reach the rainbow's end,
Give the gold to your best friend.
Save the best part just for you—
Wish on red and green and blue.

People who wish for impossible things are called rainbow-chasers by skeptics who don't believe in pots of gold. Those skeptics haven't visited the National Museum of Ireland, which is full of golden necklaces and bracelets buried by the early Celts and discovered in bogs, centuries later, by astonished peat-cutters.

The west of Ireland also happens to have more rainbows than just about anyplace else on earth. Maybe it

was just luck, but maybe peat-cutters simply knew a thing or two about chasing rainbows.

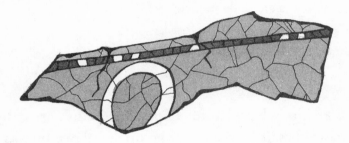

Gold or no gold, every rainbow is worth a wish. If a miracle of such unlikely beauty is possible, surely anything you wish for must be, too. Rainbows promise hope for sunny days and the sweet smell of ozone after a thunderstorm. Rainbows also bring hope for long lives, as Noah discovered after God set a rainbow in a cloud after the Flood. Noah

58

stuck around another 350 years, which is as close to living happily ever after as anyone might wish for.

When you see a rainbow, turn around three times if you think it helps, spit over your left shoulder if you must, but never, ever point at a rainbow when you're making a wish. It's guaranteed to bring the rain back again faster than you can say "Judy Garland."

Not all rainbows qualify as legitimate candidates for wishing. Rainbows in waterfalls are worth a try if you see them by accident, but don't count on rainbows you make with your garden hose because you've had a wish on your mind all day and can't wait another minute for a first star to come to your rescue. Making your own rainbow is like buying a white horse—bought wishes are all but worthless.

Four-leaf Clovers

Grant the wish fifteen times over
That I wish upon this clover.

Say it if you want, but don't get your hopes up.

Wishes, like lottery tickets, can only be used once. Besides, anything wished for to excess is bound to be bad for you, whether it's fifteen pieces of New York cheesecake or fifteen Rocky sequels. Moderation in wishing, as in life, is the golden rule.

Considering the ratio of three-leaf to four-leaf clovers in any clover patch, you'll be lucky to get even one wish, let alone fifteen. Technique is everything here. To find a four-leaf clover, you need the patience of a Buddhist monk

awaiting enlightenment. The harder you look for it, the more you don't see it. Yet the moment you stop trying, there it'll be, right in front of your eyes. Sound familiar?

Now that you have the clover in your sights, you have to decide what to do with it. This is a major dilemma, and you'll need to sit down and have a picnic so you can think it over.

Clover wishers are a nit-pickety bunch who constantly argue with each other about the right way to wish on a four-leaf clover. There are approximately forty-seven theories, the most popular of which are:

1. Over-the-Shoulder:
Throw the four-leaf clover over your left shoulder as if it means nothing to you. You'll lose it, of course, but you'll get your wish.

2. Into-the-Shoe:

Put it in your shoe, and your wish will come true when you

take it out. This theory doesn't take account of the fact that people often wear their shoes, grinding any clover inside into unrecognizable chunks of chlorophyll.

3. Into-Your-Mouth:
Horses eat clover because they're nuts about it. Humans eat it to make sure no one else will find the clover and steal their wish.

4. Leave-It-Be:
This theory has been gaining popularity recently among sustainable-clover advocates. The premise is that your wish will grow as the clover grows.

Clover wishers take these matters very seriously, and debate them every June at the International Clover Convention at Cloverfields, South Dakota. After the clover-spitting contests and the three-leaf clover races, the Clover Wishers Society meets to share tales of biggest wishes come true and discuss the finer points of clover wishing lore.

On one point they all agree: it's very bad luck to find two four-leafed clovers. If you find one four-leafed clover, make a wish, and quit while you're ahead.

The high esteem in which clover is held goes back a long way. Eve was said to have left Eden with a four-leaf clover in hand to remind her of happier times in paradise. In medieval times, the sign of the cross on the four-leaf clover was supposed to be effective in keeping witches away. More recent attempts to use it to deter telephone solicitors and junk mail have met with less success.

Dandelion Puffs

Serious wishers would as soon mow their lawns as sweep the moon and stars from the sky. The universe wasn't meant to be neat. Neither is grass, whose true purpose is to sprout galaxies of clover and dandelions. To wishers, a weed-free lawn is like an empty bank account.

When a dandelion goes to seed and turns to a white halo, it's ripe for wishing. If you can blow the whole puff off in one breath, you're a natural windbag and your wish will come true this year. If you can't, you'll never be a politician, but you won't lose your wish. The number of blows it takes you is the number of years it will take for your wish to come true.

In a recent study in controlled conditions, the average among 475 volunteers was 3.7 breaths to blow dandelion heads bare and 3.5 years before wishes came true.

A serious threat to the dandelion wisher is getting a dandelion seed in the eye, so never blow into the wind. Always practice safe wishing. There's no doubt that wishing can be a risky activity, but reports of its dangers are often exaggerated. As hazardous activities go, wishing falls somewhere between snooker and snoring.

Like any other form of wishing, dandelion puff blowing takes years of practice to perfect. The ideal training program consists of a rigorous regimen of birthday candle blowouts. Do this at least once a year, and add one candle each time, just as if you were adding weights to a barbell. In practically no time, you'll be ready to blow a dandelion puff in one breath.

Seeds in the Wind

It's a lazy August afternoon in the meadow. Summer is heavy and ripe, teetering towards the harvest moon. The air is full of silent voyagers—the seeds of thistles and milkweed and dandelions, drifting to a new frontier.

To make a wish, let one of these seeds float into the palm of your hand—grabbing is strictly forbidden. Make a wish and blow the seed away. If it floats back up into the air and stays aloft, your wish will come true. If it falls to the ground, you're out of luck. And if you fall to the ground while dancing around backwards with your palm in the air, wish for a soft landing.

Pennies

A penny saved is a penny earned, but best of all is a penny found, for it brings you a wish as long as you give it away. For added insurance, spit on the penny before you hand it over.

There once was a time when the gift of a penny was treated with enthusiasm, in the days when it would buy three blackballs or (earlier still) send a letter round the world. Nowadays, your generosity is more likely to be rewarded with a withering look, especially if you give your penny to a teenager who has been bugging you all day for a couple of thousand pennies to get a CD. The look is a price you will gladly pay if it's all that stands between you and a wish come true.

Robins

We wish on robins because they symbolize hope and charity. Hope because they're the first sign of spring in parts

of North America where winter gets to be a very ugly word come February or March. Charity because the robin was supposed to have gotten its red breast by plucking a thorn from Christ's crown and being stained by His blood. (This was actually a European robin, which is no relation to the American robin—another technicality which may be

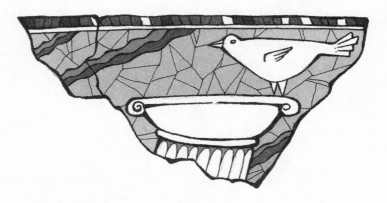

72

ignored for wishing purposes.)

As for faith, that's where you come into the picture. Without faith, your wish won't come true. Whether it comes true when you wish on a robin depends on what you and the robin do. If you see a robin perched on a branch, you should throw three kisses or count to ten while you make your wish. If you can do this before the robin takes flight, your wish may come true, but only if the robin flies up. If the robin flies down to the ground to grab the first worm of spring, your wish is done for.

If you live in an area without robins, take heart. Other red birds such as tanagers and cardinals are also good for a wish.

Black Cats

Human beings have figured out many mysteries over the last few million years, but the mind of the cat isn't one of them. Dogs are artless, transparent creatures who could no more hide a thought than pass up a soup-bone. Not so the cat, whose gaze is so inscrutable you never really know whether it's fixing to lick your hand or scratch out your eyes.

Cats unsettle us, and none more so than black cats. We've never been able to make up our minds whether to revere them or fear them. In ancient Egypt, black cats were so holy that to kill one even by accident was a crime punishable by death. By medieval times, they had become so unholy in Europe that they were thought to be witches in disguise.

With a history like this, it's hardly surprising that superstitions about black cats are confusing. Here's how it works. If a black cat crosses your path, that's bad luck. But if a black cat comes towards you, that's good luck—unless the cat changes its mind and moves away again. If the cat comes back and sidles up to you, you're in luck again and can make a wish while stroking the cat. Just make sure you stroke the front half of the cat (good luck) and not the back half (bad luck).

If you can't stand the uncertainty, get a black lab instead. You won't get any wishes, but all the wishes you grant will be rewarded with a long moony gaze of unconditional love—a concept unknown to cats of any color.

5

ON THE ROAD

Wishes can take the boredom out of driving from Topeka to Toronto or on any other long and lonely road. A kid who's looking for one-eyed cars and hay trucks is a kid who will

never again utter the dreaded words, "Are we there yet?"

Driving over Bridges

Wishes are a useful supplement to your St. Christopher charm for ensuring a safe trip. Anyone who wishes while driving over a bridge is almost guaranteed to get to the other side without the bridge collapsing.

To get your wish, all you have to do is hold your breath from one side of the bridge to the other. If you can do that for five minutes, you'll be ready to take on anything that engineers have to offer. Training is the key. Swimming the length of a pool underwater will prepare you for small bridges, but you'll need a more strenuous program to tackle anything over a half-mile long

in rush hour. Tuba lessons are the answer. Once you can play "The Flight of the Bumblebee" in under a minute, you should be ready for the Brooklyn Bridge, or even the Golden Gate.

You may wonder why, if people make wishes because they're worried about bridges collapsing, there are no guidelines for making wishes on planes. Good question— simple answer. People don't wish on planes. They pray.

Driving under Bridges

Wishing under bridges is a snap as long as you're agile and not easily embarrassed. There are three ways of doing it. Take your pick.

1. Cross the first two fingers on both hands, cross your hands above your head, and touch the inside of the car roof. Do not alarm your passengers by trying this if you're at the wheel.
2. Close your eyes, hold your breath, and throw a kiss over your left shoulder after you've passed under the bridge.
3. With one hand on the roof of the car, honk the horn with your other hand. This will cause the family dog to put its head out the window and bark three times.

If you've ever wondered why traffic under bridges gets congested; there's your answer.

Tunnels

Follow the same practice as when driving over a bridge. If anyone tries to talk to you while you're holding your breath, flap your arms. They'll get the message. (Whether it's the one you want them to get is another question.)

Railroad Crossings

Whoever thought this one up is anybody's guess, but it happens on every railroad from the Santa Fe to the Trans-Siberian.

When your car passes over the tracks, lift up both feet in the air, touch your forefinger to your tongue and then to

the car ceiling, and make a wish.

Don't be surprised if your passenger appears restless, especially after what you did at the last underpass. They may even offer a comment, such as, "Let me out of here." However hard it may seem, resist the temptation to reply. Your wish won't come true if you say a word or look behind you before you turn a corner.

Parents who live on the plains or prairies often tell this wish to their children, some of whom have been known to remain speechless for miles.

Freight Trains

One person's obstacle is another's opportunity. If you're blocked at the tracks by a slow-moving freight train with

147 boxcars, seize the moment and enjoy the view.

First, make a wish on the locomotive. Then, count the cars by saying "yes," "no," "maybe so." If the train is really clipping along, just pick up the pace—

yesnomaybeso yesnomaybeso.

The last car will tell you whether the wish you made on the locomotive will come true—yes, no, or maybe so.

Border Crossings

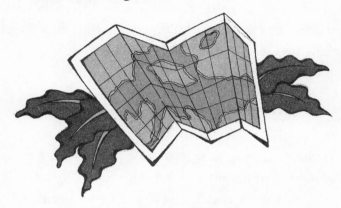

The border lines between states, provinces, and countries are like railroad tracks without the tracks. Lift your feet off the floor of the car, make a wish, and don't look back till you turn a corner.

If there's no sign to tell you exactly where the line is,

you may have to try it a few times till you get it right. If you get pulled over by an intrigued police officer, be as co-operative as you can without telling your wish. Buy time by explaining that it's a trade secret.

One-eyed Cars

If you're driving at night and see a car with only one headlight, the first person to shout "Pa-diddle!" gets a wish.

This is a wish that has always caused problems for people who like the inside of their car to be meticulously clean. "Pa-diddle!" is a word that calls for caution, especially if your mouth is full of chocolate milkshake. If there are kids in the back seat with gum in their mouths, expect to see it splattered on the windshield. Try to be philosophical about

this. There are moments in life where kids have to act first and swallow later, and this is one of them.

Some people say this wish will only come true if you also pinch the person next to you. Others say a kiss is better than a pinch. This is the option preferred in driving school, where safety always comes first.

Any wish involving math can cause confusion, which is why some people make a wish and kiss the driver when they see a car with two headlights. Fortunately, the rules of wishing are flexible on this subject. The most important thing is that you believe your wish will come true. If kissing the driver helps, so much the better.

Counting Cars

Pick out a passing car at random. If it's a Volkswagen Bug, for example, turn the ring on your finger every time you see another Volkswagen Bug. When you have turned your ring thirty-two times, you can make a wish.

88

Postscript for parents only: Lend them your rings, if you have to. This one is guaranteed to keep them occupied for at least ninety minutes. For added effect, plant the suggestion that the wish won't come true unless absolute silence is maintained till all thirty-two cars have been seen.

Hay Trucks

Load of hay,
load of hay,
Take my wish
and go away.

Whatever you do, don't look back at the hay truck after you make your wish. Not even in the rearview mirror.

Not even if there are six white horses browsing in the hay. Remember Lot's wife. She's the one who looked back at Sodom and Gomorrah and turned into a pillar of salt, which wasn't even close to her wish.

Tradition has it that you can't look back at a hay truck because a death will occur somewhere if you do. A death will occur somewhere no matter what you do, but that's beside the point. The reason a death is supposed to occur is that hay represents the transitoriness of all life. As far as the Grim Reaper is concerned, we're all fields of hay when he sharpens his scythe. If it's any consolation, grass always grows back after it's cut down. Maybe you will too. Make hay while the sun shines, and make wishes while the hay truck passes.

If the load of hay is already baled, you won't get your wish till the bales are broken. As this could be in January, wish for something that can wait awhile, like a spring romance.

90

Mail Trucks

You can go for months without seeing a hay truck in the city. Not to worry. Wishing on a mail truck is just as good, as long as you don't look back. If you do, your wish won't come true and the mail truck will bring you a pile of bills, a check in your name for a million dollars that turns to dust when you read the fine print, and an invitation to purchase a rowing machine.

In Scotland, a stopped mail van was an invitation for school children to race to touch the picture of the crown on the side. The first one to do so got a wish, the second a kiss, the third a disappointment.

Wells

While driving, keep your eyes peeled for a well, but steer clear of lawns with plastic ones. Wishing on a fake well will only get you a fake wish.

Real wells are a different story. They're magical, through and through. Some of them, like the one at Lourdes, even bring miracles. Wish on them for all you're worth.

Wishers used to drop crooked pins into wells—when the pin reached the bottom of the well, the wish would

come true. The pins were offerings to the water gods who lived in wells and kept the precious, life-giving water flowing. Why people thought water gods liked having pins dropped on them is anybody's guess, but a tradition's a tradition.

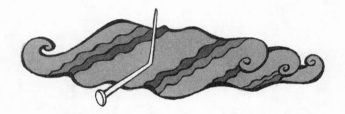

Some fairy-tale characters didn't stop at pins—they dropped themselves into wells, wishing for eternal life, convinced that where there's a well, there's a way.

Wells are few and far between these days. So are

93

crooked pins, and anyone with eternal life hasn't been talking about it—not even to Geraldo.

If you can't find a well, substitute a fountain. If you're fresh out of crooked pins, a coin will do. Stand with your back to the fountain and toss the coin over your left shoulder.

Some well wishers believed that it helped to make a favorable impression on the water gods by crawling three times around the well in the direction of the sun. If you do this at a fountain in a mall, the water gods will be highly entertained. So will the rest of the shoppers. If you can't figure out which direction the sun is moving, ask the mall security guards. They will probably be so helpful, they'll insist on taking you outside so you can see for yourself which way the sun is moving.

6

HOME, SWEET HOME

When you've come home after a long day's wishing, chances are you'll be hungry and tired, ready for a hearty meal and an early night. Conveniently, most indoor wishes are related

to eating and sleeping.

With the right combination of rainbows, white horses, and one-eyed cars, all your wishes may have already come true. This will cause you a moment of sudden, uncontrolled despair until it hits you that you can never run out of wishes. It's like running out of love. Impossible.

First Visit

The first time you enter anyone's home, walk in backward and make a wish. This will help break the ice and will also let your host know that you're someone out of the ordinary. More importantly, your wish will clear out any malicious spirits that might bear you ill will. In medieval

times, walking backward was supposed to confuse the devil, presumably because the devil had a habit of lurking behind people's left shoulders and would trip if forced to walk backward on his cloven hooves.

For the same reason, walk in backward and wish whenever you move to a new home. Do this before carrying in the bride or bridegroom, if you have one with you. Dropping your spouse as you trip over the threshold is no way to start a marriage, even if your wish comes true.

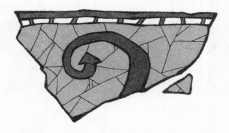

Going to Bed

Considering that we spend a third of our lives asleep, it's hardly surprising that beds occupy a large place in wishlore. The wishes that have been invented through the centuries to ensure sweet dreams and a safe waking are imaginative and varied. If you make all of them, you'll be busy till well past your bedtime.

The first night in your new house, or whenever you

sleep in a strange bed, name the four corners of your bed (North, South, East, West, or Sarah, James, Dorothy, and Bill, depending on your preference and sense of direction). Then close your eyes, make a wish on each corner, and turn around three times. The corner that you look at first after you've opened your eyes (if you're still upright) will be the corner on which the wish will come true.

The second night, and every night after that, turn your pillow over three times and make a wish.

Some people believe you can get a wish by kissing the right leg of whatever stuffed animal you sleep with. If you sleep with a stuffed elephant or any other four-legged creature, wish on its back right leg.

If you have no stuffed animals, a human leg will do, if there's one in the bed with you. Kisses on legs work best for short-term wishes. If yours doesn't come true immediately,

try kissing other body parts till you get the desired result.

Alternatively, you might find yourself merely wishing your kids would go to sleep. Don't bother. Dream the impossible dream if you want, but don't waste time wishing the impossible wish.

Once all these wishes are made, you will sleep as sound as a baby. Wishing is the best cure for insomnia, and the wish you're thinking of when you fall asleep is the one most likely to come true.

102

Dishrags

Not as romantic as a falling star, but still not a wish to be sneezed at (or on). It goes like this: if you drop a dishrag, step over it backwards, and make a wish.

Some people say that dropping a dishrag is unlucky and that the only way to get your luck back is to bury the rag in the light of the moon. This rule was most likely invented by a 12th century teenager trying to escape his chores. All superstitions you hear from teenagers should be taken with a grain of salt. The most reliable sources of information about wishes and all superstitions are people under 12 or over 70. Anyone in between is prone to making things up.

Speaking at the Same Time

You're in a boardroom meeting, everyone's talking at once, and you and someone else say exactly the same words at the same time. Call an immediate adjournment—you've just earned a wish, and this will take a while.

Make sure you get this right. Link your right baby finger with the right baby finger of the other person and make a wish. With your fingers linked and eyes closed, the two of you must now have a conversation consisting entirely of pairs, something like this:

You:	*Needles.*
Other:	*Pins.*
You:	*Triplets.*
Other:	*Twins.*
You:	*Salt.*
Other:	*Pepper.*
You:	*Gin.*
Other:	*Tonic.*

Carry this on till you can't stand it anymore, and finish up like this:

You:	*What goes up the chimney?*
Other:	*Smoke.*
You:	*I wish this wish...*
Other:	*...will never be broke.*

With your fingers still linked, press your right thumbs together and say together:

> *Pinky to pinky, thumb to thumb,*
> *Wish a wish and it's sure to come.*
> *If yours comes true,*
> *Mine will come true.*
> *Pinky to pinky, thumb to thumb.*

That's it. You'll have good luck, both your wishes will come true, and the whole thing will be recorded in the minutes to prove you did it right.

You should do the same thing if you're walking hand in hand with a friend and get separated. The first item of business when you come back together is a wish and the ritual of the pinkies.

There's a shorter form of this ceremony if you forget the right words or don't have all day. In this version, each of you says the name of a different poet. Any poet will do except Shakespeare, who spears your wish, or Burns, who burns it. Then one of you says, "I wish, I wish your wish comes true," and the other says "I wish, I wish the same for you." This mutual generosity will make you friends for life—or at least for fifteen seconds.

Then there's the instant version, for those in a real hurry. Whoever says first, "Buy me a beer" or "Jinx, you owe me a Coke" gets it—and their wish.

Striking Clocks

If a clock strikes (indoors or outdoors) at the moment you're making a wish, the wish will come true. Some wishers

say that the beeping of a digital watch will also make your wish come true, but this claim has yet to be verified.

One thing's for sure. Planning a wish for 2 p.m. and scheduling it in your appointment book will get you nowhere. You might as well try to plan a shooting star, for all the good it'll do you. Serendipity is the cardinal rule for all wishes.

7

Food, Glorious Food

Some people wish to eat, others eat to wish. The best part about wishing on food is that it's right there on your plate, and the rules aren't complicated. You don't have to crane

your neck looking for something to wish on. You don't need to turn around three times. And you don't have to avoid looking at your cake after you've wished on it, unless that's the only way you can stick to your diet.

Salt

Salt was as precious as gold in the days when it was used to pay Roman soldiers their salaries. And, as a symbol of vitality, it was put in coffins to keep away the devil, who hated the sight of it. Spilled salt, however, was great news for the devil and bad luck for everyone else. That's why Leonardo da Vinci's painting of the Last Supper shows Judas knocking over the salt shaker.

If you spill salt at dinner, don't even wait to finish your sentence. Grab a pinch of it and throw it over your left shoulder. This will temporarily blind the devil, and give you a chance to make a wish.

If you feel self-conscious doing this, consider the alternative. According to early folklore, those who neglected to throw spilled salt over their shoulder were doomed to come back after they died and pick it up with their eyelashes. You would not enjoy this. Don't chance it.

113

Tea

Bubble, bubble, toil and trouble,
Make my wish true, on the double.

The magical powers of tea date back to its origins at about 500 A.D., when a monk by the name of Bodidharma cut off his eyelids to allow him to contemplate Buddha without being interrupted by sleep. He flung the eyelids to the ground where, to the surprise of contemporary botanists, they sprang into plants whose leaves produced a drink that banished weariness.

The other great benefit of drinking tea is the wish you get when you stir it. When you remove the spoon, the bubbles clustered at the middle of the cup will wander around aimlessly for a while, and just when you think

they're about to pop, they'll suddenly slide over to a point on the rim. Whoever they're pointing at, gets a wish.

If this isn't you, drink your tea and brew up another pot. If necessary, be prepared to follow the example of Cornelius Bontekoe, the 17th century Dutch physician, a serious tea-drinker who claimed to drink up to 200 cups of tea every day. This left him little time to see patients, but he never ran short of wishes or of urologists with a keen interest in his career.

Eggs

Eating a boiled egg without salt and pepper is like kissing a man without a mustache, according to men with mustaches. You won't spill the salt or sneeze on the pepper, but the egg will taste bland. On the other hand, it may have a double yolk.

It's hard to lay a double-yolk egg when you're feeling

depressed. That's why hens who spend their lives in cages rarely do it. Free-range hens, who get to eat worms and grubs, get as elated as one can reasonably be in a state of chickenhood, and frequently lay double-yolk eggs. Every one you eat, with or without salt, will grant you a wish.

The second reason to raise hens in your backyard is that the first egg laid by a pullet is also good for a wish. If the pullet saves this feat for Easter Day, make three wishes.

In Kansas, it is said, you can make a wish by throwing a pullet's egg over a building. You may wish to see who's over there before you do this. On the other hand, all kinds of strange things happen in the skies over Kansas. Anyone being hit by an egg there is likely to assume it's just a leftover from a tornado and carry on about their business.

Wishbones

Every bird has one, whether it's a chicken, a turkey, or an ostrich. It's that little forked bone between the neck and the breast, and it's the best part of Thanksgiving.

Some ancient seers used to divine the future by examining the entrails of birds. Modern prophets have abandoned this practice in favor of other equally reliable but less stomach-turning techniques. The only modern reminder of entrail-reading is the wishbone, which predicts the future perfectly by making wishes come true.

118

Let it dry. Don't hide it somewhere as you're bound to lose it. Some people say that if you hang a wishbone over a doorway, you'll get a wish every time you walk under it.

After you've spent a few days working out the details of the wish you want to make, find a willing partner. Hold out a pinky, grab an end of the wishbone, and pull till it snaps. Longest end gets the wish.

Apples

This requires a sharp knife and dexterity. If you can peel the entire skin off in one continuous strip, make a wish. To make it come true, turn around three times and throw the peel over your left shoulder.

As an added bonus, the shape of the fallen peel will tell you the first letter of your true love's name. This is useful if a) you have a true love but they aren't ready to tell you their name, or b) you don't have a true love but you've been reading entrails and foresee one heading your way.

Pieces of Pie

If it's not your birthday, forget cake. Order pie. Lemon meringue, maple pecan, blueberry; it doesn't matter what kind.

If the point is served towards you, you get one wish. Needless to say, it won't come true if you served the pie to yourself. No wish can survive a conflict of interest.

Your second wish comes when you're ready to eat the piece of pie. Cut off the point and push it to one side of your plate. Eat the rest of the piece while you seriously consider your wish. Eat the ice cream while you make sure it's really the wish you want. Then put the point of the pie in your mouth and make a wish before you swallow it. Turn the plate around three times to make sure your wish comes true.

If the restaurant in which you're playing with your pie is truly elegant and you are truly hungry, put the empty plate on your head. In international pie language, this means, "More pie, please." There's no better way to show your appreciation and get another plateful of wishes.

Birthday Cakes

Birthday cake, birthday cake,
Give me every wish I make.
If I don't blow every flame,
Give me wishes all the same.

Everyone knows this one. Blowing out candles on birthday cakes is one of the oldest and best-known wishing rituals of all. In ancient Greece, worshippers of Artemis, the goddess of the moon, would place honey cakes on the altars of her temple to celebrate her birthday, which

like the full moon came once a month. The
cakes were shaped like the full moon and
were lit with tapers. If her worshippers
could blow out the flames in one
breath, Artemis would gaze
favorably on them.

A favorable gaze has its
advantages, but a wish-come-true delivers the goods. By the
Middle Ages, German parents were putting candles on their
children's birthday cakes, with a candle for each year and an
extra one to represent the light of life. Just like today, the
wish came true as long as it wasn't told and the candles were
blown out with one breath.

If you don't blow out all the candles at once, you'll still
get your wish eventually, but you'll have to wait the same
number of years as the number of candles you missed. For

124

your wish to come true this year, you have to get all the candles with one breath.

Before you blow, invite everyone present to put a ring on a candle. The owner of each ring around a blown-out candle will get a wish. Watch where the love of your life puts his or her ring so you can blow that candle out first. This is a must if the love of your life is still holding onto your birthday present.

If you're a risk-taker and hate getting your wishes easily, hold onto your ring till the candles have been blown out, then put your ring on a candle with an ember still glowing in the wick. If that's the last ember to die out, you'll get your wish.

Now cut the cake and make another wish. If the knife comes out clean, that wish will come true too, as long as you don't say a word till you've eaten your piece of cake.

8

FROM HEAD TO TOE

We're always losing bits of ourselves—teeth and eyelashes and nose-hairs and such. Most people don't worry obsessively about such things in the last decade of the 20th

127

century—they save their anxiety for serious concerns like wrinkles and gray hair. It was a different story in the days when feuds were settled with black magic instead of Saturday Night specials. Whoever possessed your toenails and other abandoned parts had the basic ingredients needed to cast spells against you. Wishing on the lost bits began as a way of practicing some positive magic to counteract such malicious enchantments.

Clothing and jewelry were less likely to go missing, so wishes on them tended to be inspired by symbolic attributes, like the perfection of the shape of the ring, or the chaos of inside-out clothes.

Lost Teeth

Whoever lost a tooth in medieval times would conceal it to keep it out of the clutches of practitioners of black magic. Then, one day, some enterprising six-year-old hid a tooth under a pillow; and the rest, as they say, is history. The Tooth Fairy has been practicing her own brand of magic for many generations, transforming lost teeth into pieces of silver.

If for some reason the Tooth Fairy doesn't come—or if you'd rather get a wish than a coin—throw the tooth backwards over your left shoulder. Your wish will come true if you can't find the tooth after you throw it. The best place to do this is in a clover patch the next time you go looking for four-leaf clovers.

If a mouse finds the tooth instead, so much the better—your new tooth will grow in as hard and sharp as the mouse's. At least, this was the theory that led to the European tradition of hiding teeth in mouse and rat holes. This is only an advantage up to the age of eight. If you're growing sharp new teeth at twenty-six or forty-three, consult your physician or, better yet, a theatrical agent. You could have a promising future in bad horror movies.

Lost Eyelashes

For some reason, eye-
lashes are attracted to bowls of
soup, and that's where you're most
likely to find yours. Put it on the back of
your left hand (the eyelash, not the soup); then,
put the back of your right hand under the palm of
your left. Move the salt shaker to a safe distance. Now, hit
your left palm with your right hand three times, close your
eyes, and make a wish.

If the eyelash is still on your hand, you won't get your
wish. But if it has disappeared or fallen back into the soup, it
has gone to get your wish. Even better, your soup will have
cooled off, and you won't have to blow on it.

To prepare yourself, study your eyelashes carefully in

131

the mirror. That way you won't mistake the waiter's eyelash for your own. Wishing on someone else's eyelash, no matter how long and attractive it may be, is a waste of time. So is wishing on false eyelashes.

Fingernails

Take a look at your fingernails. If one has a white spot underneath, you're probably not getting enough zinc in your diet.

This is a medical question either to save for your doctor or else ignore as one of many symptoms you would never have noticed if someone hadn't brought it to your attention. You've survived so far, haven't you? The important thing to do right now is make a wish. When the white spot grows out, your wish will come true.

Sneezes

If you spill the pepper, don't waste it by throwing it over your shoulder. Sprinkle it on the palm of your hand, put your nostrils very close, and breathe in gently. This will produce a faint tickling in the nose followed by an ecstatic moment of suspense, and should not be done at dinner unless you are on the most intimate terms with your companions.

There are few greater pleasures in life than a good sneeze, or four, if you really let loose. The wish that comes with it is the gravy, metaphorically speaking.

You can wish on sneezes two ways. If you believe, as many used to do, that your soul flies out when you sneeze, make a wish beforehand so that you won't sneeze. By the time you get around to doing this, the horses will already be heading out of the corral and you'll be well launched into your second and third sneezes. Enjoy them. With any luck,

some alert person a couple of blocks away will hear the commotion and shout "Gesundheit!" This will restore your soul and your good health, too.

The Romans, who knew how to enjoy life, believed that sneezes were lucky because they expelled evil spirits, not souls. This explains why some people make a wish after they sneeze. Such a wish will make sure the evil spirits stay out and attach themselves to someone else who needs them more than you do.

Remember, also, that whatever you're thinking about when someone (you or anybody else) sneezes, will come true. That's why Penelope sighed with relief when her son Telemachus let fly with a mighty sneeze. She was wishing for the safe return of Ulysses from the wine-dark seas, and guess who showed up for dinner? Always think good thoughts and you'll have nothing to worry about.

135

Inside-Out Clothes

Clothes manufacturers sew on a label so you'll know which is the front and which side goes inside. This is a help, but if you're half-asleep and it's dark and you're late and you've left your wits in bed, it may not be enough.

What usually happens is that some kindly soul takes you aside around 11 a.m. and reminds you that your sweater or shirt or sock is inside out or backwards. Thank them for their thoughtfulness, and leave things be. To discover that you're wearing your clothes inside out or backwards is not only very good luck, it's also good for a wish—as long as you keep wearing them inside out or backwards for the rest of the day. Appearances are important, but why waste the chance to make what just may be the wish of a lifetime?

Rings

The circle is the perfect shape, unbroken and without end. That's why the bride and groom exchange wedding rings as a symbol of eternal union.

Any ring you wear will protect you from bad luck, and whoever presents the ring to you can give you a bonus by sliding it onto your finger, turning it three times towards your heart, and making a secret wish on your behalf. Leave the ring on as long as the giver tells you, and your wish will come true when you take it off.

Necklaces

Clasps of necklaces have a way of slipping from the back of your neck to your throat. This will be noticed not by you, but by the same friend who always discreetly reminds you, depending on your sex, that your slip is showing, your fly is at half-mast, your clothes are inside-out, or your socks don't match when they're actually meant to.

Ask this observant and helpful person to move the clasp of your necklace to the back of your neck while you close your eyes and make a wish. From now on, the universe will unfold as it should, and your wish will come true.

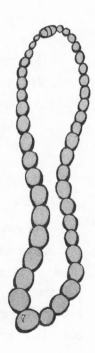

138

Shoelaces

If your shoelaces come undone during the day, this is bad luck, and not just because your chances of tripping are greater than usual. The good news is that you get a wish, but only if someone else ties up your laces for you.

Children, through some kind of mysterious magic, can undo their shoelaces within fifteen seconds of having them done up, without even touching them. Children, unlike adults, seem immune to bad luck, perhaps because they have the sense not to believe in it. They only believe in wishing, and take every opportunity to make wishes on undone shoelaces and everything else under the sun.

9

THROUGHOUT THE YEAR

Before the days of year-round greens in supermarkets, the turning of the seasons was far more important to people than it is today. The beginning and ending of each was a cause for

141

celebration or mourning, and the ceremonies marking those times naturally included the ceremony of wishing, which in some cases has evolved in curious and wonderful ways.

First Day of the Month

You can get a wish the first day of every month, but you have to prepare for it the night before. Whatever you say after your head hits the pillow, your last words before you fall asleep must be "Black Rabbit! Black Rabbit! Black Rabbit!"

When you wake up the following morning, on the first day of the month, pinch and punch anyone in your bed, and shout, "Pinch, punch, first day of the month!" Then, say "White Rabbit!" three times and make a wish. Depending

on the temper of the person you pinched and punched, you'll have good luck all month long. Do this every month, beginning in January, and your year will be blessed from beginning to end.

First Sign of Spring

Sometime around the middle of February, soon after Groundhog Day, people who not so long ago wished for a white Christmas, start wishing never to see another

143

snowflake or drop of rain ever again. Wishes made at this time of year often feature white shell beaches and endless summers, for spring is a non-committal season. It has an infuriating habit of sticking its nose in the door and then backing out and disappearing for a few more weeks. The good news is that you can wish on any sign of spring, the first time you see it.

Some people aren't convinced that spring is really on the way till they see a robin, but pussy willows and sunning snakes and honey bees and a hundred other things are good for wishes, too. All that matters is that it's the first you've seen this year.

First Day of May

In past centuries, far more attention was paid to the first of May than was ever given to the first of January. In pre-Christian times, Celtic peoples divided the year at the beginning of summer and winter: on May 1 and November 1. May meant the return of warmth and light and, most important of all, food in the belly as the growing season began. May Day became one of the great festivals of the year, including mock battles between revelers dressed up as Summer and Winter. (Summer always won, much to everybody's relief).

May was also the month for planting the seeds of love. In 19th century Edinburgh, throngs of young women would gather to wash their faces in the dew before sunrise on the first day of May. Not only would dew magically give them perfect complexions, but a wish made for a certain person to become a sweetheart was supposed to come true.

Irish maidens also went out at sunrise on May Day, but to a different destination—the nearest well. The belief was that if you gazed into the well on this particular morning, you would see the reflection of the face of your lover, and whatever wish you made (presumably for your lover to appear in the flesh) would come true.

If you're fortunate enough to have indoor plumbing, you'll be hard-pressed to find a well to gaze into. Searching at dawn for the reflection of your lover's face in the bathroom faucet may lack the romance of old, but if you truly believe...well, who knows? It may be worth a try if you're already up, on your way outdoors, to wash your face in the dew.

First Fruit of Summer

Strawberry, raspberry, apple, pear. Whatever the fruit is, if it's fresh and it's the first of that kind you've tasted this year, make a wish the moment you take your first bite.

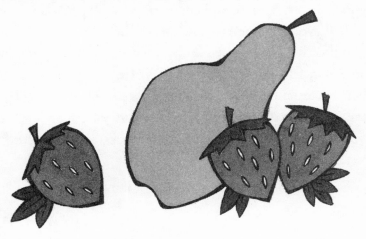

August Meteor Showers

When summer gets huge and over-ripe, teetering into the time of the harvest moon, it may briefly cross your mind that winter may someday return. This troubling thought can be easily forgotten in the second week of August, when the Perseid showers hurl shooting stars through the heavens at the rate of more than one a minute. These stars all come from the same part of the sky. If you imagine the sky as a huge bathtub, with the stars hurtling out the plug hole (this may tax the imagination more than you like), then the plug hole is the constellation Perseus, near Cassiopeia, the goddess whose throne of stars resembles a giant W.

Astronomers will tell you that the Perseid showers are tiny bits of rock and dust and ice thrown into the atmos-

phere by the Swift-Tuttle comet when it makes its yearly visit. Let them think what they want. You know a shooting star when you see one. Watching the Perseid showers is as close as you'll ever come to having stardust sprinkled in your eyes, and you'll make enough wishes to last you a month of Sundays.

Halloween

Among Celtic peoples, Halloween was a day to remember not only the dying season but also the souls of those who had died that year and would return this night to revisit their old homes. Centuries later, witches were believed to go galloping through the countryside on tabby-

cats transformed into coal-black steeds. Huge bonfires were lit so people could keep an eye out for these and other prowling spirits. You never knew who or what was likely to come knocking at your door.

The wind always seems to rise at Halloween, moaning through the trees like a disembodied baseball fan who's just watched his team lose the last game of the World Series. This makes it a prime night for wishers who wander abroad, trying to catch falling leaves.

Catching a falling leaf in a breeze is no mean feat. If you don't have the stamina and agility of a ten-year-old, think twice about even trying. Falling leaves have a way of slip-sliding away from your outstretched hand, especially when you're keeping an eye out for wandering spirits.

Each leaf you catch is worth a wish, and some say that if you catch 365 falling leaves, you'll get a whole year's worth of wishes. Others, who know how hard it is to catch even one leaf, say each leaf counts a month, and you only need twelve. Either way, expect to stay outside a long time.

Christmas

If you're part of a family where Christmas puddings are a tradition, don't miss your chance to stir the batter. Do it three times, wishing all the while and stirring hard enough so you can see the bottom of the bowl. Whether or not

you'll need to lick the spoon to make your wish come true is something you'll need to decide for yourself. The practice of magic is a very personal affair.

If brandy is poured over the pudding and set on fire, the pudding will light up with everyone's wishes as it's carried to the table.

If you come from a rice-pudding rather than a plum-pudding family, the rules are slightly different. It takes a very eccentric cook to set fire to a rice pudding. What most cooks do instead is put a single almond in the pudding. Whoever gets it in their serving, also gets a wish.

New Year's Eve

As an alternative to making New Year's resolutions, write all the wishes you can think of on separate pieces of paper. When you go to bed, stuff the pieces under your pillow, and don't forget to say, "Black Rabbit" before you doze off.

When you wake up in the morning, as soon as you've said, "White Rabbit," reach under your pillow and pick out a piece of paper. That's the wish that will come true this New Year.

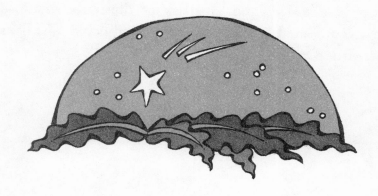

David Greer is a writer and lawyer who lives in Victoria, British Columbia.

Chum McLeod is an artist and illustrator whose work has appeared in many magazines and books. She lives in Barrie, Ontario.

If you liked *White Horses and Shooting Stars* chances are you'll enjoy Conari Press' other titles, including *Slowing Down in a Speeded Up World* and *Random Acts of Kindness*. Call or write for a catalog:

Conari Press
1144 65th St. Suite B
Emeryville, CA 94608
(800) 685-9595